The only thing Divot and Swish love as much as playing sports is eating ice cream.

After a fun week at sports camp in the Ozark Mountains, they headed to Happy Cones. Divot ordered a cup of vanilla with sprinkles on top. Swish chose two scoops of strawberry in a waffle cone.

They sat at a patio table topped with a big red umbrella. Their pets, Kali the puppy and Lennie the lizard, sat next to them begging for a bite.

They happily ate their ice cream and watched people ride by on brightly colored bikes. There were parents helping their toddlers ride balance bikes without pedals. There were families on city bikes made for riding in town. And there were riders on mountain bikes, hybrid bikes, and bikes built for two.

As they were leaving Happy Cones, Divot and Swish stopped to look at a shiny blue and orange mountain bike.

Just then a friendly voice said, "Hi! I'm McKenna the Mountain Biker, but you can call me Kenna."

They looked up to see a girl with a rainbow sherbet cone walking toward them.

"What are your names?" she asked.

"My name is Divot, and
Swish is my best friend.
Our pets, Kali and Lennie,
Are also our friends."

"It's nice to meet you all!
I saw you with my bike outside,
And it made me curious
If you two like to ride?"

With enthusiasm, Swish said,
   "I like riding my bike
     At our nearby state park.
     I meet my friends there
     And ride trails that are marked."

"What about you, Divot?" Kenna asked.
   "I have a bike at home
     And ride sometimes to school.
     But I go very slowly
     And follow all the rules."

Kenna offered,
   "If you're in town tomorrow,
     My family owns a bike shop.
     I could take you for a ride
     And show you both a lot."

Divot and Swish looked at Kali and Lennie, who were barking and chirping with excitement.

Swish paused and politely asked, "Can we bring Kali and Lennie with us?"

Kenna answered, "Of course!"

"I'm in!" hollered Swish.

But Divot wasn't so sure. She didn't have as much confidence in her biking skills as Swish did.

Just talking about biking made Divot feel anxious. She remembered the kids who laughed at her the last time she rode to school.

"I'm not too sure I want to ride.
Maybe I could go hiking.
Because other kids have teased me
For not being good at biking."

Kenna responded with encouragement,
"You may not be good at biking YET!
But the only way you'll improve
Is to practice your skills,
Whether you win or you lose.
See, creating your confidence
Is something you can choose."

"Please," Swish pleaded with Divot.
"Okay," Divot reluctantly agreed. She didn't
want to let her best friend down. Plus, Kenna
seemed nice and would be there to help.

"I'll meet you in the morning
At Ozarks Family Bikes.
My dad and I will be there,
And we open at first light."

The next morning Divot and Swish walked into Ozarks Family Bikes. Kenna was waiting for them with a smile. They were amazed by the number of brilliant bikes that were standing in neat rows and hanging on the walls.

"Let's find some mountain bikes that fit you," Kenna said.

She walked toward a row of kids' bikes and selected one for each of them. She also helped Divot pick out a purple helmet that fit snugly over her golf visor. Swish found a shiny blue helmet that matched the stripes on his basketball shoes.

After they loaded up, Kenna led them to
a grassy area behind the bike shop. Divot
and Swish stared wide-eyed at the smooth
green surface dotted with yellow cones and
lined with yellow rope.

"It looks like a maze," said Divot.

"This is our biking course," explained
Kenna. "It's a safe place to practice."

She pointed toward a blue sign and said,
   "Start here and keep your eyes
    Looking where you want to go.
   Ride between the yellow cones
    Whatever pace—fast or slow."

While Swish rode his bike confidently through the course, Divot fell behind. She was feeling frustrated and almost quit several times.

Then Divot remembered what Kenna had said yesterday. She started repeating to herself, "I may not be good at biking YET, but I'll get better if I keep practicing!"

Kali also encouraged Divot with friendly barks and tail-wags as they approached the end of the course.

Kenna cheered,
"Great job, Divot, going at
Your own speed!
And was that you talking, with
Kali following your lead?"

"Yes!" Divot responded with more certainty.

Turning to Swish, Kenna said,
"I enjoyed watching you ride
With your passion and your flow.
And I noticed you kept looking
Where you wanted to go."

After celebrating, they all walked across the grass to the paved bike path.

Kenna explained,
"To be safe on the paved path
Stay to the right of the lines.
Both on paved paths and trails
Use your voice as a sign.

If you're slowing, shout 'slowing!'
If you're stopping, let us know.
If you're passing a rider,
Call out 'passing' as you go!"

Feeling overwhelmed, Swish said,
"I don't feel very confident
When I need to speak out loud.
Mostly, I feel nervous
Especially in a crowd."

"That's interesting," replied Kenna.
"You just need more practice
Creating confidence in your voice.
When it's important to speak,
Tell yourself it's your choice."

"Let's keep practicing as we head to the mountain bike trail," she suggested.

"How big is the mountain?" Divot asked nervously.

Kenna replied, "We'll start on beginner trails that are smooth and flat."

Swish asked,
   "But Kenna, what about me?
   I want to ride something tough.
   I'm really good at biking, and
   Those trails won't be hard enough!"

Kenna told Swish he could soon ride faster and take trails with bigger rocks and hills to climb. That sounded good to Swish, but Divot still had her doubts.

With Kenna leading the way, they soon left the paved bike path behind and entered the mountain bike trail.

Divot was pedaling slowly and passing the All-American trail sign. Suddenly she felt a bump from behind, and something knocked her to the ground!

Kenna jumped off her bike and ran toward Divot, shouting, "Are you okay?!"

"I think so," Divot said, as she looked up and adjusted her helmet. "Kali seems to be okay too. What happened?"

Swish spoke up,
    "I'm so sorry Divot.
     I tried to go around
     But didn't call out 'passing'
     And knocked you to the ground."

"It's all right, Swish," replied Divot.

Then Kenna encouraged Swish,
    "Continue to stay focused on
    The skills that you're improving.
    Don't compare yourself to others
    But just to how you're doing."

"Does that mean NOT to compare myself to Swish when I'm biking?" Divot asked.

"Correct," responded Kenna. "And Swish can do the same."

"Right," chuckled Swish. "Because if I compare myself to Divot, I'll never believe I'm good at using my voice."

"Now you're both getting the hang of creating your confidence!" said Kenna joyfully.

She guided them over a wooden bridge as the wildlife watched them approach a shaded trail.

Swish went faster and took the steeper, rockier trails. Jumping off the dirt and rock ramps thrilled both Swish and Lennie, and they couldn't wait to find more!

Divot started slower and stayed on the easier trails that had small climbs. But the more she rode and kept her eyes focused on the trail, the faster she and Kali went.

They heard Kenna's voice through the trees calling, "Watch for the signs ahead and follow them to Ho-wa-e-li-s-di Falls!"

When they reached the falls, they leaned their
bikes against two giant oaks and stood next
to Kenna. Water poured over the huge rocks
and splashed into a clear blue pool below.

They saw fish relaxing at the water's edge,
frogs lounging on lily pads, and turtles resting
in the sun. Even the squirrels and rabbits
stopped playing to watch the waterfall.

"What does *ho-wa-e-li-s-di* mean?"
Swish asked curiously.

Kenna shared,
   "In the Cherokee language,
   Ho-wa-e-li-s-di means confidence.
   Which you've been creating
   With me as your audience.

   Also, it's the perfect place
   To take a break and say,
   What has been most fun for you
   On our adventure today?"

Swish replied with a smile,
"The challenging trails
Have been the most fun for me.
And when I get nervous
Using my voice is the key."

Divot chimed in,
"I enjoyed improving
My bike-riding skills
And I know that with practice
I'll gain confidence on hills."

"That's right!" exclaimed Kenna, sharing their joy. "Confidence is your superpower because you can create it!"

As Divot and Swish pedaled happily back to the bike shop, they thought about what their new friend, McKenna the Mountain Biker, had said. They knew it wouldn't be easy, but they were ready to head home and have fun creating their confidence.

Adventures with Divot & Swish in the Ozark Mountains would not be possible without the support and assistance of so many people.

I am deeply thankful to Dad, Martha, Andrea Shea, and Dana for their continuing encouragement.

To Letty, who challenged me early in my writing journey to move in a more playful direction.

To my sidekicks, Andrea and Lauren, for their dedication to the website and publicizing the Divot & Swish series.

To Cole, Donna, and Sheila, who shared their expertise in the Cherokee language.

To the staff at Buchanan Bicycles for their expert technical advice.

And to all those who read and critiqued multiple drafts of this book:

Gentry, Graysen, and Samuel

Julie and Full Circle Bookstore

Denise

Elle, Amberly, Adelyn, and Jackson

Amy and Julia

Kari and Izzy

Rae Lynn and Audrey

Juliana, Jim, Malcom, and Lukas

MJ and Lillian Grace

Dewayne, Davis, and Della

and Ryan, Gina, Rosa, and Lua.

Published by Divot & Swish Publishing | Norman, OK

ISBN13: 978-1-7351700-3-9

Illustrations by Charlotte Strickland
Cover and interior design by Carl Brune
Editing by Alice Stanton

Project coordination by Jenkins Group, Inc. | www.jenkinsgroupinc.com

Printed in the United States of America by Jostens Commercial Printing.

First Printing, September 2021, #78243

25 24 23 22 21 • 5 4 3 2 1